6

 7

 8

 9

 10

 16

 17

 18

 19

 20

 26

 27

 28

 29

 30

 36

 37

 38

 39

 40

 46

 47

 48

 49

 50

 56

 57

 58

 59

 60

Michael Hall

Monkey Time

GREENWILLOW BOOKS

An Imprint of HarperCollinsPublishers

Pssst! Wake up, Monkey!
It's time to play.

Wheee! I bet you can't catch a minute, Monkey.

Chase me
over.

Chase me
down.

Chase me
all the way
around.

Faster,
Monkey,
faster.

Hop! Pop!

Ha-ha. You missed me.

Look, Monkey.
There goes another minute.
Can you catch that one?

Chase it over. Chase it down.
Chase it all the way . . .

Pop! That one got away from you, too!

We are lightning fast,
and you are a slowpoke, Monkey.

Pop! Three
minutes have
slipped away.

Pop! Four.
Pop! Five minutes
have passed.

Pop, pop,
pop, pop!
Six, seven,
eight, nine.

Pop! Ten.

We're running circles
around you, Monkey!

Pippity-pop! Pippity-pop!

Pippity-pippity-pippity . . .

Our hour is almost over.
There's only one minute left!

Chase it
over.

Chase it
down.

Chase it
all . . .

Wait!
Hold on!
Did you . . .

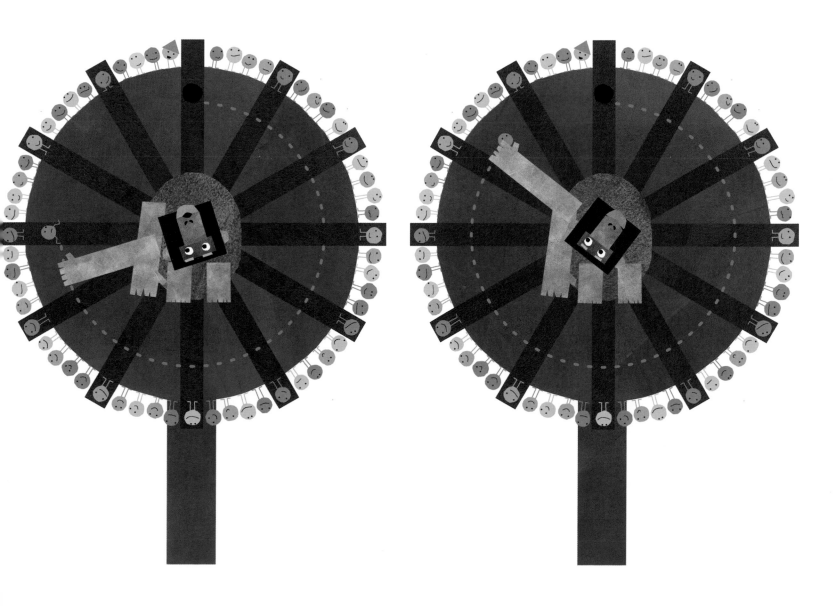

You did it!

You caught a minute, Monkey.

Just in the nick of time.

I didn't
think it was
possible.

Ummm,
Monkey?

Now that you have a minute, what will you do with it?

Whoa! Don't do that!

Pop!

Ahhh!

Thanks, Monkey.

Wooosh!

Good-bye,
Monkey.

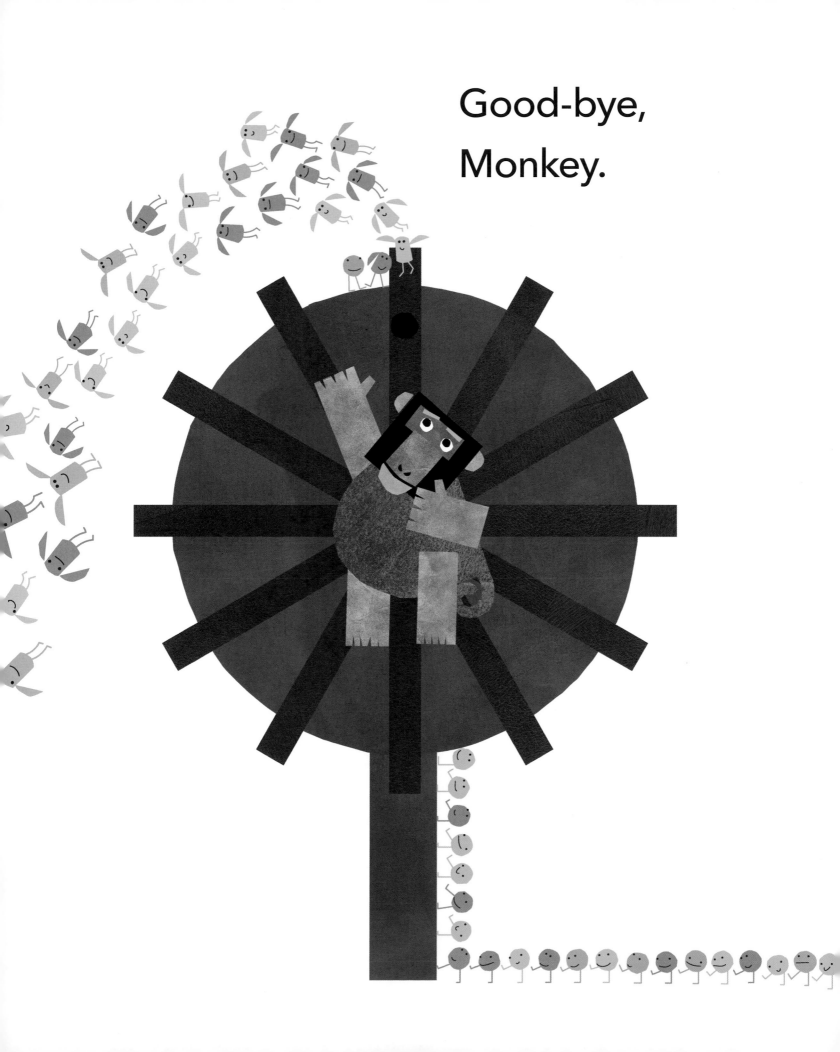

Pssst, Monkey.

Guess what time it is?

Monkey's Rainforest Friends

The animals in this book live in or near tropical rainforests around the world. Tropical rainforests are ecosystems clustered near the equator. These dense jungles are home to many different trees, plants, insects, birds, reptiles, and other animals.

Tonkean Macaque Monkey
Indonesia

There are many kinds of macaque monkeys. Their primary source of food is fruit. Some eat leaves, bark, and seeds. There are no reports of macaques eating minutes.

Chameleon
Africa, Asia, Australia, South America

A chameleon can fling its sticky tongue at an insect several feet away, capture it, and pull it into its mouth in less than a second. If you blink, you'll miss it. What does the chameleon in this book eat?

Three-Toed Sloth
Central and South America

Sloths are slow-moving animals. When on the ground, they can take two minutes to travel the length of a car. A human baby can easily crawl twice as fast. Sloths spend most of their time in trees. Usually they climb down only once a week, to poop! How far does the sloth in this story travel?

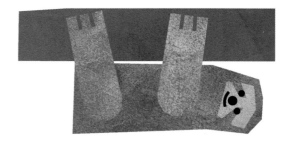

Green Tree Python
New Guinea, Indonesia, and Australia

Most snakes can stretch their mouths like a rubber band to swallow animals that are quite large. It can take a snake more than one hour to swallow a meal and weeks to digest it. What does the green tree python in Monkey's forest eat?

Scarlet Ibis
**South America
and Caribbean**

The scarlet ibis probes for food in shallow marshes, under sand, and beneath plants. Scientists think that its bright red plumage is the result of its diet of crabs and shrimp.

Crimson Finch
Australia

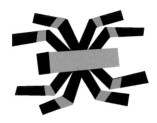

It can take a crimson finch chick an hour or more to peck and push its way out of its shell.

Poison Dart Frogs
Central and South America

Many rainforest animals, such as chameleons and mantises, blend into their surroundings. They use camouflage to hide and protect themselves. The deadly poison dart frogs use color to stand out. Their distinctive colors warn predators to stay away.

Golden Orb-Weaving Spider
Primarily Africa, Asia, and Australia

The golden orb-weaving spider can spin a web in thirty minutes to sixty minutes. Then it waits at the center of the huge web for insects to become stuck in the sticky strands.

Praying Mantis
Temperate, subtropical, and tropical areas all over the world

Praying mantises are skilled hunters. Often difficult to see among leaves, they can strike an insect in less than a second. Did you spot the insect this one ate?

Morning Glories
Worldwide

Most morning glories blossom in the morning when the sun rises. The flowers fall off the vines later in the day and are replaced by new blossoms the next morning.

Minutes
Worldwide

The minutes in Monkey's forest gather in sets of sixty and keep track of time passing.

Keeping Track of Monkey's Time

Every hour has exactly
60 minutes in it. Monkey
can't count to 60 yet, so
Monkey keeps track of time
by watching the circle of
minutes in his tree fill up.
When the whole circle is full
of minutes, that means an
hour is over.

Measuring Time

60 seconds = 1 minute

60 minutes = 1 hour

24 hours = 1 day

What can you do . . .

in a second?

in a minute?

in an hour?

in a day?

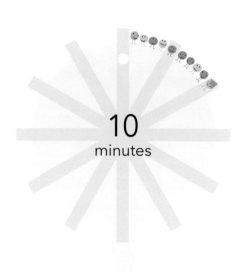

10 minutes

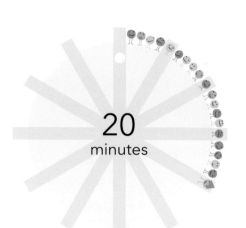

20 minutes

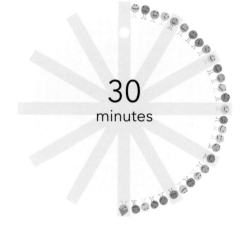

30 minutes

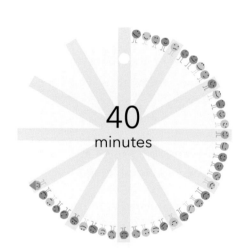

40 minutes

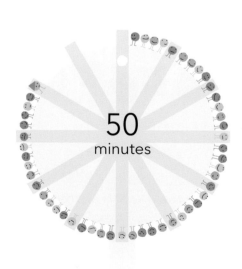

50 minutes

60 minutes

For Aunt Franny

Monkey Time
Copyright © 2019 by Michael Hall
All rights reserved. Manufactured in China.
For information address HarperCollins Children's Books,
a division of HarperCollins Publishers, 195 Broadway,
New York, NY 10007.
www.harpercollinschildrens.com

The art consists of digitally combined collages
of painted and cut paper.
The text type is 30-point Avenir Next.

Library of Congress Cataloging-in-Publication Data is available.
ISBN 978-0-06-238302-0 (hardback)

19 20 21 22 23 SCP 10 9 8 7 6 5 4 3 2 1
First Edition

 Greenwillow Books

1

2

3

4

5

11

12

13

14

15

21

22

23

24

25

31

32

33

34

35

41

42

43

44

45

51

52

53

54

55